THE END OF TIME IS HERE DASHAVTAR AND 2012

lucifer

First Published in March 2022

ISBN: 978-93-5611-448-7

BLUEROSE PUBLISHERS

www.bluerosepublishers.com

info@bluerosepublishers.com

+91 8882 898 898

Cover Design:

Muskan Sachdeva

Typographic Design:

Ilma

Distributed by: BlueRose, Amazon, Flipkart

Dedication

This book is dedicated to free thinkers, rationalists and people who are not afraid to ask questions. This book is also dedicated to the people who believe in one Supreme power that flows through all life.

Acknowledgement

I would first like to thank my parents for the values and freedom of thought that was given to me since childhood. My friends for their patience to listen to all the ideas that popped in my head. My family for supporting me through my tough times. The great thinkers, philosophers, men of reasoning of every time and every culture whose words or thoughts have guided me in this life.

Preface

What makes me qualified to write such a book is a natural question that should be thought of by everyone before reading this book. The answer to that question is my ability to think about a question which no one has thought of and the answer I have given to those questions in this book. Apart from my findings in this book, I have no achievements to brag about. However my stories will definitely make you question your blind beliefs and of those around you.

Foreword

I know the author of the book as Rohit Gaikwad. I have known him since his birth. His father, Rajendra Gaikwad was a student of mine. Rajendra is like a brother to my children. His parents Rajendra and Vasudha are like extended family to me. When Vasudha asked me to write this foreword I couldn't say no. I have read this book for the purposes of proofreading. Being an English professor my main reason to read was to correct grammatical errors. I couldn't catch all the ideas that were tossed in the book. So, Rohit and I had a long chat about the ideas he has written and frankly they are a little revolutionary.

The book he has written is a little difficult to read. He has tried to find logic in the mythological stories of the 10 avatars of Vishnu. The ideas are really different from what you expect out of a book written on the Dashavatar stories. If you read them with an open mind, I am sure you will find them interesting. It took me a lot of time to grasp the sense he was trying to make, but most of them looked logical, and do tend to make sense. Now it's upon you to decide what you just toss away and what to believe in.

- Dr. Shubhangi Sitaram Raykar

(Former Professor at Fergusson College, Pune)

Index

Introduction 1
MATSYA (Fish) 11
Kurma (Tortoise) 15
Varaha (Boar) 23
Narasimha (half lion and half man) 28
Vamana (the Pygmy man) 33
Parshuram (the first immortal) 37
Ram (the ideal man) 43
Krushna (the perfect man) 54
Buddha (the peace bringer) 67
Kalaki (The last man standing) 79
Author Introduction 89

Introduction

I was planning on writing a book on each avatar separately, so as to study all in detail as it will be difficult to accept all at once but Covid19 has forced my hand to compress all in one, should anything happen to me the knowledge might not see the end of light. I just have one request, read it with an open mind, and I am sure it will blow your mind away. Many of you might have reservations or down right oppose some of the concepts mentioned in the book, let that not stop you from finishing this book. Also I may have made some mistakes. It's quite possible as I am just a human and not an avatar of God.

The holy Trinity of Indian gods is Brahma, Vishnu and Shiva. Brahma signifies creation, Vishnu signifies Preservation and Shiva signifies destruction. The word GOD itself is an acronym for Giver, Observer and Destroyer. Brahma is the name given to the energy of the creation. Similarly Vishnu is a name given to the energy that conserves this universe. Shiva the destroyer is the almighty God >1. There are stories we will further understand that will mention Vishnu and Brahma to be Shiva devotees. There are 10 avatars of Vishnu. It is said that Vishnu took many other partial forms but the

10 were the major forms of Vishnu >2. That is because they signify the important stages of the evolution of life. We will study the 10 forms thoroughly, through which we will understand the evolution, the meaning and the goal of human life. Along with that some basic understanding of our concepts will be challenged, the meaning of some of your day to day words and phrases will be questioned and reevaluated.

I started this journey on a simple set of rules on the guidance of the great astrophysicist and TV presenter Neil deGrasse Tyson. These sets of rules were followed by generations of scientists before. Quoting Tyson the set of rules is quite simple "test ideas by experiment and observation, build on the ideas that pass the test, discard ideas that fail, follow the evidence wherever it leads and question everything". Now a logical question should arise in our minds like how Dashavtar and evolution of life are connected. One is part of ancient Indian mythology and the other one is the backbone of modern scientific ideology. The connection was made by Helena Blavatsky, a great theoretician of Theosophy. She was also one of the founding members of the Theosophical Society. She wrote about the uncanny similarity between Dashavtar and Darwin's theory of evolution in her books Isis unveiled, which was published in 1877 >3. It was a brilliant example of pattern recognition. The theosophical society, founded in 1875 in New York by Blavatsky and her associates, found no takers in the western scientific society. The headquarters was shifted to Madras. Blavatsky died in 1891.

When you see Dashavtar through the prism of evolution, great new information can be found in the stories and forms of the avatars. It's not like we haven't figured out the small details individually. We already have all the clues with us. Hidden in our arts, literature, movies, science and even in our everyday life. All that is left to do is the menial task of connecting the dots. In the book I have used art and movies to emphasize on some of the points and also to draw reference. A fraction of knowledge of Ramayana and Mahabharata that is needed to understand the 7th Avatar, Ram and the 8th Avatar, Krishna is given, but the interpretation of these great epics have varied through centuries. I have tried to see the evidence of these great epics individually, with no previous prejudice and by isolating some incidents. All we have to do is question the stories to get our answers. To quote Einstein "imagination is more important than knowledge". Imagination is the language of our soul. Instinct and imagination are the 2 tools that have guided me to these answers.

To challenge any thought or idea we have to use the tools of questioning. Namely who, what, when, where, why, which and how. All the major religions ask us to have faith and abandon questioning. This in turn obstructs us from questioning their ideas and philosophy, which may have been relevant at the time of their inception but some of them at least are completely irrelevant today.

For example an experiment was carried out on 5 monkeys who were put in a cage. A ladder was kept in the middle of the cage and bananas were placed on top of it. Anytime a monkey went to take the bananas cold water shower was poured in the cage before they could reach the bananas. The monkeys tried again and again but every time someone touched the ladder there was an intense cold shower. The monkeys slowly observed the cause of the rains and stopped trying to get the bananas. If a monkey was tempted the others stopped it by beating. One day one monkey was replaced with a new one. The new one naturally went for the bananas but the other monkeys stopped it by beating, in a way asserting their seniority. The new one was obviously bamboozled but was forced by peer pressure. Now the new monkey was subconsciously programmed, that climbing the ladder will get beating from the other monkeys. Then one day another monkey was replaced. Again, the new one was naturally tempted and again the other monkeys stopped it by force not letting him touch the ladder. The first new monkey now under peer pressure stopped the second one as well, not knowing the reason but just submitting to peer pressure. Slowly all the old monkeys were replaced by new ones but the tradition continued. Not knowing why it was done but just following peer pressure. Later even though the rains were stopped the traditions didn't. Similarly in every culture there is a reason for the traditions. We seldom ask the reason for our culture and tradition. Most of us follow the festivals of our culture for the enjoyment of breaking the routine of our lives. Let's awaken ourselves to reality and illuminate the light of knowledge. And in the process we will all be Illuminati, the illuminated ones.

Now let us ask the basic questions to the Dashavtar theory and find answers to many questions like how did life evolve, how did animals evolve from life, how did humans evolve from animals. The ancient knowledge lost in the sands of time survived in stone. Today various civilizations have merged into a new age of technology. Looking through the prism of dashavtar, we can see the images of the end of time in 2012.

What exactly is the Dashavtar?

If you ask any common Indian this question they will tell that these are the 10 incarnations of Supreme God Vishnu. Most of them won't even be able to tell you the names of the 10 avtars. But allow me to tell you that sometime in the past they compiled 10 avatars of Vishnu, the energy of preservation. These avatars have their stories and forms. While studying the avatars we will understand it's meaning and symbolism through 2 ways, the form of the Avatar and the story behind it.

When was it decided that these are the 10 avatars of Vishnu? Ashoka and his nine men are a long lost conspiracy that could be connected, but without any solid proof we can only speculate about it. Any new concept will always take time for acceptance. But it was the Gupta regime 5 centuries later when it was widely propagated. The dashavtara temple was the first Vishnu temple built in India. However the name Vishnu is present in 5 of the total of 1028 verses of the Rig Veda written roughly around 300 BCE>4. However, this also falls just as Alexander's victory over king Porus, which was around 328 BCE>5.

Why did we compile the Dashavtar?

Rig Vedas were hymned for a very long period of time before they were finally written down. Alexander the Great launching an attack on the Indian subcontinent could have been a very motivational factor to write down the Rig Vedas, which were transmitted in verbal manner before that. Chanakya knew that if Alexander would have conquered India and ruled here for some time, he would have changed the very ways of life, understanding and beliefs. Just like all the conquerors did before and after that. All this important knowledge could have been lost in the sands of time. The Middle East and Europeans invaded India after these avatars were compiled and Aryans invaded before. The Aryan invasion though was not mere territorial but more of an intellectual kind. Even wars were fought in the name of god at that time. The Indian crusades were fought between Vaishnavas, the followers of Vishnu and the Shaivas, the followers of Shiva. The followers believed that Vishnu and Shiva respectively were the greatest of the holy Trinity. The Vaishnavas won the wars. Hence Vishnu then became the Supreme God we know him today as.

Who compiled it is an interesting question. Alexander came calling 100 years after Buddha. We can safely assume India must have been on the cusp of the then dominant Buddhist philosophy of nonviolence. Hence we were in a very vulnerable state. Chanakya went to great lengths to avoid it. Hence it is safe to assume that the people who did this went at great lengths to safeguard it. The 10 avatars of Vishnu compiled for Vishnu Gupta or commonly known as Chanakya himself could be a good speculation. King Asoka and his nine men could have done this as a tribute to Vishnu Gupta.

How it was compiled is a very difficult task and can only be speculated. Ashoka and his nine men could have created the stories or made subtle changes to the existing popular stories to suit the narrative. It is easier to understand how it was spread. The Gupta Empire emerged from the ruins of the declining Mauryan empire around 2 centuries after the fall of Mauryan empire and roughly 5 centuries after the reign of Asoka the great. The Dashavatara temple was the symbol of the Gupta dynasty >6. They were Vaishnavas, who preached the Vishnu theory. We can safely assume that it was during their rule that the festivals having Vishnu related stories were made common. I am not saying they started it but it was made common during the time. The roots of the current Indian culture and way of life lie in the Mauryan and the Gupta period, which is considered as the golden period of Indian history. Comparative study can be made from recent history. Just like the European renaissance period laid the foundation of modern day American dominance.

In the Dashavtar the stories are superimposed over the knowledge to transmit the knowledge for a longer period of time. Just like in radio technology the shorter sampling frequency is superimposed on the larger Carrier frequency >7. This phenomenon helps to transmit messages over long distances in space. The dashavatar stories create a message which travels a long distance in time until now. The knowledge at that time was transferred by word of mouth only from a teacher to the student. I hope all are familiar with the game of Chinese whispers, so as to understand what happens when information is carried by word of mouth. Because of the superimposition of stories over the knowledge the distortion caused to the original knowledge is less. It is still slightly distorted by the people who sometimes made changes to the stories but many times didn't even understand the original message. A slight deviation, sometimes to suit their own propaganda, sometimes to keep it relative to changing ways of time and sometimes to change the nature of the story. These changes were also made to hide a fact considered sacrilegious with the changing time. Slowly the slight deviation accumulated, sometimes leading to the loss of the original message as well.

Where were the avatars compiled? It's possible that the answer to this question can be lost in sands of time. The rise of the Gupta period also coincides with the rise of the great learning centers. Universities like Nalanda and Takshashila became great learning centers of the world. People from different parts of the world came to study at these Universities. These students would have brought in their culture and stories with them as well. Evidence does suggest the presence of these universities from before the Gupta period, however evidence also suggests that these universities reached their peak during the same time as that of the Gupta's >8. The social model of society might have changed at these universities. Slowly and steadily the effects were reflected in the society, namely the resurgence of the caste system, Sati system, which became more common during this time >9. Initially the caste system may have helped the Guptas to reach the heights they achieved. But the long term effects led to the division of the people, which further led to a long term rule of the subcontinent by external forces. The rise of these external forces started with the Ghori's, the Khilji's in 12th and 13th century CE, followed by Tughlaq's, the Lodi's, the Mughals afterwards, up until the British Raj which ended in 1947 CE >10. Now let's move on to the last question.

Which are the 10 avatars of Vishnu?

The forms of Vishnu in their specific order are as follows

1. Matsya (fish)
2. Kurma (tortoise)
3. Varaha (Boar)
4. Narasimha (Lionman)
5. Vamana (the pygmy man)
6. Parshuram (the 1st immortal man)
7. Ram (the ideal man)
8. Krishna (the perfect man)
9. Buddha (the peace bringer)
10. Kalki (the last man standing)

MATSYA

(Fish)

The story

Once upon a time there lived Hayagriva. Hayagriva was the son of sage Kashyap and was the king of Danavas. He stole the knowledge of 4 Vedas from lord Brahma so as to help the danav clan and weaken the devas. Vishnu had given the Vedas to Lord Brahma for safe keeping. The people at that time were not considered pious enough to understand it and hence a purification was needed. Lord Shiva, who is the lord of destruction, under the request of lord Vishnu created a great flood. Vishnu saved Manu and his wife Shatarupa, in the form of a fish. Manu saved a pair of all the animals in the world. Manu also had the seven great sages of that time with him on the journey. A great boat was created to carry all tied to the horn of the fish. The fish navigated the boat at the time of the great flood. After the flood receded a book was written for the remembrance of time before.

Explanation

According to today's science life began in water. The form of the first avatar i.e. fish, symbolically gives out the same message. It was a way to understand that life began in water. Fish over here is used as a symbol as it is the most common and most easily relatable water life. Hence it was an apt symbol for the message.

Is it possible that it is a true story? Well yes and no. We cannot deny the possibility. Human growth has exponentially increased after the last of the ice ages. After the ice age, sea levels rose by 120 meters >11.

Maybe the rising sea levels could have alerted the humans who might have created a boat to save themselves. The story could have changed forms as people challenging the story would have raised many questions. The changes were made in the story for the knowledge to survive the logic of questions. The fact that a pair of all animals on the boat is an example of the change brought by logical questioning. It was just an answer improvised to counter the questions, "if what you say is true what about the animals?". This answer would have satisfied the believers and would have quieted any non-believers.

The part of the seven sages is a very beautiful example of how science and logic are hidden in these stories. In the above story we learned that the seven sages were also travelling with Manu. If we take it literally then it means that the seven sages were on the boat. However, the seven sages have all varied in the different puranas. The seven sages actually symbolizes the Ursa Major constellation in the sky >12. Ursa major and Ursa Minor are very important constellations in the sky. They help us locate a single star out of the millions of stars in the sky. The one star that has been used for navigation since ancient times, The north star. The north star is called "Dhruv" in Indian traditions. In the story the seven sages being with Manu, only means that Manu relied on the north star for directions during the journey, and on the constellation of the seven sages to locate Polaris.

In parts of India whales are called "dev masa" or "god fish". As it is the biggest fish that can complete the gigantic task mentioned in the story. It could have been that a large fish, maybe the last of its kind, had a horn. Which the people might have used to steer the ship. It's all speculation. The moral that we can take from this is that life began in water, which is a scientifically accepted fact of life today but a very important piece of information that was known since ancient times hidden in the Dashavtar.

Kurma

(Tortoise)

The story

Once upon a time the devas lost the control of the 3 worlds, when the Danava King Bali rose to power. The devas had suffered a curse from the great sage Durvasa. Durvasa once received a garland from an Apsara. The garland was a special one, as it was the dwelling of fortune. Durvasa decided to give the garland to Indra, the king of devas and the ruler of the 3 worlds. Indra in his attempt to show his own humility, places the garland on his mount Airavat, the elephant. Now the flower on the garland attracted some bees. Airavat threw the garland on the ground, irritated by the bee. This angered Durvasa and he cursed devas to be bereft of energy and strength. Having already lost the gift of fortune through the garland's destruction, the devas lost the 3 worlds to danava king king Bali. The devas went to Vishnu for help. He figured a direct battle was not going to help. They decided to create amrit for the devas to drink and regain their mojo. Vishnu was going to take the Avatar of the tortoise. Place mount Mandara on his back and churn the ocean of milk, the home of lord Vishnu. The ocean was to be churned with the help of the great snake Vasuki who lived on Shankar's neck. Vishnu knew that it was dangerous to hold the mouth. Devas couldn't do this task alone and needed the help of Danavas for that. Devas put forth the idea to the Danavas. On Vishnu's instruction, Devas pretended to have the right to hold the mouth of the serpent's body, as the mouth of anybody can be considered purer than the tail end part. Danavas being the rulers of the 3 worlds took it on their ego and insisted on holding the mouth. Devas gladly accepted the counter offer.

The stage was set, the players were ready. But the mountain initially refused to bulge. It was then found that both parties were pulling simultaneously. Shankar then sat on the top of the mountain and started shouting instructions. Both the parties then started working on Shankar's instruction, working in tandem. But still the mountain was unmoved. Shankar came to assist again. Shankar was well liked both by the Danavas and the Devas. Shankar went to the end of danavas and started yelling insults on the Danavas. Danavas used that anger to pull the mouth of Vasuki. Vasuki in the pain of the tension on his body bit many Danavas. The poison of the Vasuki was lethal, hence killing many Danavas in the end. Shankar then shouted similar insults on the devas, who in turn focused their anger on pulling the tail. This anger helped to break the inertia. And whenever the devas or the danavas got tired Shankar would shout to motivate both the parties. But still nothing happened. Due to constant shouting Halahal the poison then slowly started to appear on Shankar's throat. The constant shouting had turned the throat blue.

Now the fruits of the labour slowly started to emerge from the ocean. First came Lakshmi the goddess of prosperity. She accepted Vishnu as her consort. Then came the various apsaras. They went to the Gandharvas (The clan that functioned as artists of heaven). Gandharvas used to entertain the gods in Heaven. So apsaras invariably went to the devas. The last apsara was Varuni, who was argumentative in nature, and was hence given to the Danavas.

Then came Kamadhenu, the first cow. Kamadhenu is the mother of all cows. She is a wish granting cow who was given to the saptarishis, the great 7 saints. Her milk and the ghee were useful to the saints in their Yajnas. Then came Uchhashravas, the divine 7 headed horse, which was given to the Danava king Bali. After the fall of Bali, Indra took the horse.

Then came Kalpavriksha, the eternal wish granting tree. Parijata, the divine flowering tree whose flowers would never wilt, came next. Devas took both to heaven. Then came Kaustubha, the most valuable jewel of the time, Shranaga, a powerful bow and Shankha, the coonch were next to come out. All 3 were given to Vishnu. At last Dhanvantari the heavenly physician came with Amrita, the eternal elixir. The Devas and the Danavas both fought for the elixir. Garuda, the great eagle, was the vahana (vehicle) of Vishnu. He took the pot in his talons and flew away taking the elixir with him. The amrita got spilled at 4 places on Earth. They later became the 4 places where the Kumbhmela took place. But the danavas were weakened by the Vasuki, many danavas lost their life to its poison. Lord Vishnu then took the form of Mohini, a beautiful damsel, to distract the Danavas. Mohini was then tasked with distributing the Amrita. Mohini cleverly distributed the amrita so that no Danavas could get it. But a Danava called Swarbhanu disguised himself as Deva and drank the Amrita. Vishnu cut his head with the Sudarshan chakra, his divine disk. Now the still immortal head was called Rahu and body was called Ketu. Then the Devas, having regained their mojo and the Danavas being weakened, were able to win the 3 worlds back from the Danavas.

Explanation

The form of the tortoise symbolises the terrestrial transition of life. Life in this stage transitioned from water to land. What could be a better example than tortoise? How turtles and tortoises transitioned from aquatic to terrestrial can also be imagined. Eggs can be easily hunted. Turtles lay eggs on land so as to safeguard the eggs from carnivorous aquatic animals >13. So we can assume that the original transition of life to terrestrial was just temporary, which later turned more permanent in the form of tortoise as it would have survived easily as carnivorous animals might not have been developed on land.

The symbolism of the story is much more layered. It is a formula to create something immortal. Devas is the symbol of positive energy and asuras is the symbol of negative energy. Now the physical description of the devas is of Aryan nature and that of asuras or rakshasas is of Dravidian nature.

Now understanding Amrita is very simple. It's the creation of something immortal. It needs both positive and negative energy to work together. Along with Amrita, halahal was also created, which was held by Shankar in his throat, it symbolises that the task of creating something immortal, invariably creates a poison along with it to maintain the balance. Balance, as science already explains, is at the core of the universe's existence. You can find many instances of clashes between 2 different powers. It's like a natural struggle of two powers found in all cultures, The Yin and the Yang. And in these clashes we will find the Amrita as well as the halahal. The modern day world wars caused large scale destruction, millions died. But modern day science will find its roots in the technology created by these wars and the ones before. The best example is the computer. The machine built by Englishman Alan Turing to decode the German coding machine Enigma became the first design for a stored program computer. Struggle enables us humans to achieve something beyond our normal reach.

Now Indian culture has a special place for cows. Cows give milk which is vital in the Indian food culture. Cow dung was used as a natural insecticide. Cow dung used to be placed on the walls of the houses. Even the cow urine is still thought to be pious enough to consume. This means that along with milk every other material from it is useful. So many solutions of that time came from cow products. The problem of inflation was faced by people of that time too. However they found a brilliant way to overcome that. They assigned cows as a medium of exchange of goods just like gold and copper coins. Civilizations all over the world have used cattle as money >14. This allowed relaxation of the pressure to mine more gold and copper. Copper and gold could be used in utensils, ornaments and in making beautiful temples. Now one little problem had to be dealt with before cows could be assigned as currency. The only problem with assigning cows as currency was that it was easy to kill a cow. If two men were making a struggle of power against one another then by killing cows of the other would be seen as a masterstroke. However killing cows would mean not only the death of the animal but also would be very dangerous for the economy of the nation. Hence the ban of cow killings was first instilled in the minds of the people. Now due to this the currency of the nation was always going to increase, as the cow population was always going to rise. We do find reference to cow sacrifice in early vedic literature but these traditions have faded out. Hence the importance of cows to Indian civilization. The world may make fun of India for its obsession for cows but it was the animal that provided food and pesticides. Most importantly it was the currency that made India reach the heights of economic, culture and power. Due to a large number of cows, abundance of milk and milk products became common. So we saw milk being offered to god in large quantities. It's sad to see the same rituals being continued, especially when many people are going hungry. Following these rituals and traditions without understanding its meaning is what led to the downfall of the great nation but the roots of the culture could not be cut down.

The character of Varuni, the argumentative women, is a great indication of the equal status of women in the early Dravidian or Danava culture. This symbolises the equal status of women was a concept that was core to the Danava philosophy not Devas. Devas assigned the status of goddess only to the consorts of god's. If we look more carefully we will definitely find more hidden symbolism in all the ratnas that came out of the Samudra Manthan. We just have to take the guidance of logic and science.

Varaha

(Boar)

Story 1

Once upon a time Brahma and Vishnu had a debate as to who among them was superior. While debating they came across the shivling, a long fiery lingam pillar, which stretched from the bottom of the earth to the skies. They said that they will try to find the start or the end of the pillar, and whoever does so first would be superior among them. Brahma sat on his vahan the swan and said he will find the end of the lingam pillar. Vishnu took the Boar Avatar and said he will dig in the earth and find the start of the pillar. After a long long time they were unable to find neither the end nor the start of the lingam. Brahma saw a Ketaki flower falling from heaven. He asked the Ketaki flower to come with him to Vishnu and inform him that he plucked the flower from the end of the lingam. Brahma then went to the starting place and waited for Vishnu. Shiv then taking pity on both of them took his human form and met both of them on the starting place. He explained that the lingam has no start or end and it is futile trying to find it. Then Brahma and Vishnu both accepted that indeed Shiv is the most superior of the 3.

Story 2

A long time ago a demon named Hiranyaksha dragged the earth to the bottom of the sea. Vishnu then took the Varaha avatar, slew the demon and raised the earth out of water with his tusks.

Explanation

This avtar of boar explains the modern day accepted form of evolution. The theory laid out by Darwin. The survival of the fittest was how Darwin explained it. The form of the avatar, that of the boar symbolizes survival. Even today boar is one of the widest ranging mammals in the world, next to us humans of course. Not surprisingly it has been accessed as the least concerning animal on the UN red list >15. The boar is also omnivorous like most of the humans today, which again symbolises survival.

Now the stories tell us a far more deeper meaning. The presence of the two separate stories gives us indication that there were modifications made in the later time to these stories. When a piece of knowledge is accepted and understood by all it tends to lose its value. The first story is actually a kind of a puzzle, wherein a commonly accepted knowledge today, that the universe is round, can find its root. Indians have been using the term "ye duniya gol hai", meaning the world is round, so commonly for a long time that they have lost the story from which this thought came. In the story Shiv is symbolized as a pillar. A pillar with no start and no end. "Na adi hai na ant hai uska" we can find this line mentioned in many Indian poems or even modern day songs tributed to shiva. Consider the pillar as a line, so what is a line that has no start or no end. Basically it's a loop, the circle of life. The story is inscribed in the elephanta caves near Mumbai. The same caves were damaged by both the Gujarat sultanate and the Portuguese invaders, but were not able to destroy its message >16.

Indians had found much of the knowledge independently that modern science used as a base.

Trigonometry played a vital part in the scientific revolution. Today Indians perform rituals in the name of 'Kaal Sarp Yog'. They have lost the true meaning of the term and blindly follow ancient customs. The name is made of 3 words. 'Kal', meaning time. 'Sarp', meaning reptile. And 'Yog', meaning to align together. Indians performed yogasana, meaning postures to attain yoga, for centuries. When you practice the postures of yoga your mind and your body start aligning together. So the word kalsarp yog means that time (kal) and reptile. The word 'Sarp' can be roughly translated as crawl. So animals that crawl are called sarp. Snake is the best example as its structure resembles a line. Now how exactly is that possible. The movement of a snake is in the form of a wave. The below diagram will make things crystal clear.

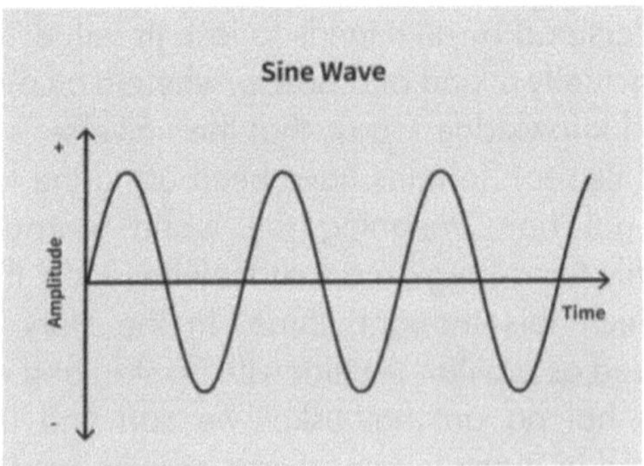

The diagram of the sinusoidal wave

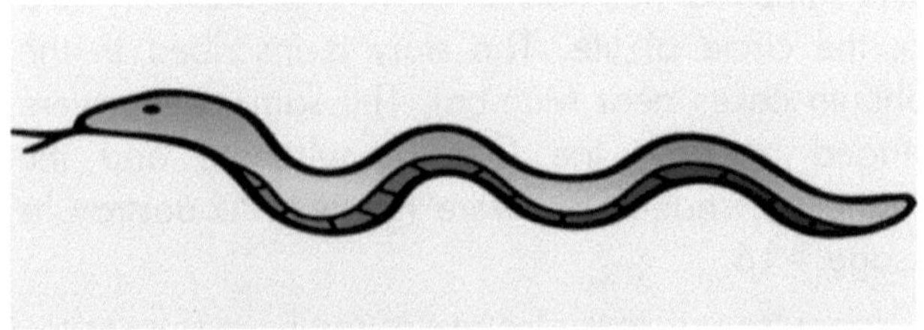

The movement of a snake (reptile)

The new story also makes an attempt to connect the avatars together. Creating a story to connect the next avatars. This attempt was to connect the avatars together in a single continuity. So that people believe in the stories of these avatars. This was done with a good intention of fooling people into believing that these are actual happenings, so that people take these stories seriously. Just like a parent cajoling their infants into eating healthy do sometimes use tricks.

The second story is of a theory I remember studying in my school geography class. All the continents were once all connected as a single mass of land called pangea >17. They drifted apart as they are today due to tectonic movement. Now there can be two possible methods of that happening. One is that they were always above ocean level and then drifted apart. The other theory, not widely accepted one, is that Pangaea was originally under water and that it rose above water as they appear today. The avatar raising it on tusks could be a symbolism, that the land rose above water as they are and were all once part of the same land mass. This is just a speculation, but that's what we can narrow it down to.

Narasimha

(half lion and half man)

The story

Once upon a time there was a demon king named Hiranyakashyap. He had a son named Pralhad. Prahlad was a devotee of Vishnu. Hiranyakashyap hated Vishnu as he had killed his brother hiranyaksha in his varaha avatar. Now Hiranyakashyap tried to kill his son Prahlad multiple times. His sister, Holika, had a boon that she would not be consumed by fire, basically she was fireproof. Prahlad sat on a pyre with her and due to Vishnu's grace Prahlad came out unhurt but holika died. The reason Indians celebrate Holi till today. Hiranyakashyap was still not satisfied and tried multiple other ways to kill his own son. Just like holika who had a boon, Hiranyakashyap had a boon too it was that he will not be killed by a man or an animal, he will not be killed by any weapon or instrument, he will not be killed in day or night, he will not be killed in his house or outside his house, will not be killed in heaven or hell. Then one day Hiranyakashyap asked Prahlad if there is a god Vishnu then he asked where is he? Prahlad replied that the god is everywhere. He asked if the god was in a pillar in his palace. Prahlad replied yes god is everywhere. Hiranyakashyap broke the pillar with his mace. Out of the pillar came the Narasimha avatar of Vishnu. He took Hiranyakashyap to the door of his house, so he was neither inside nor outside. He placed Hiranyakashyap on his lap. Now Narasimha was half man half lion, so he was neither a man nor an animal. It was evening time that Narasimha appeared, so it was neither day nor night. Hiranyakashyap was killed by the nails of narasimha avatar so no weapons or instruments were used to kill him. He was killed on earth so it was neither heaven nor hell. So came the end of the evil Hiranyakashyap.

Explanation

Now in the chronology of the Vishnu avatars this avatar comes after animals and before all the human avatars. Even the crux of the story is the boon of Hiranyakashyap. Neither here nor there, somewhere in between. This story actually answers the question of how we became human. God is a power, "Shiv hi shakti hai". If we analyse carefully every religion gives us a similar image of God, the all-knowing all-powerful being. But is God really a being or just an energy? We believe god created humans in his own image, isn't it just the opposite we created god in our own image, something we can relate to. Hence Greeks have Zeus, Egyptians have Ra. Even cosmic entities like the sun, moon, even the wind and fire have been humanized in almost every culture, this is because of the lack of explanation of these natural phenomena at that time. This proves that humans have personified gods and other natural powers in their mythological stories. With the rise of modern scientific thinking, we have left these beliefs in the past. God in the true capacity is a power we can never fully understand however much we try to. If we match the descriptions of god, isn't a god similar to dark energy? An energy which if assumed answers questions but we have failed for concrete evidence for both, someday hopefully we might succeed. An energy which is going to be the reason for the destruction of the universe. Shiv, Allah, God, dark energy whatever we choose to call that it's an energy that defines the balance of the universe. So how does the story help us understand the relationship between human and god? Well the story is of the very old debate of an atheist and a believer. Hiranyakashyap asked similar questions to Prahlad, what an atheist would ask a believer even today. So we became human when we understood that there is a higher power. God made us human when we constructed the idea of God. In almost all the cultures we find an entity which is symbolised as god. To make it a little simpler, let's consider another famous question. Did man create god or god created man? We became humans from animals when we felt gratitude for the gifts bestowed on us by nature. We created God to project that feeling of gratitude. So God created man when man created god. For example we can safely assume today that there is no god named Ra. And it was just a symbol dedicated to the sun. But imagine trying to say that to a common Egyptian when pyramids were being built, I am sure we would get the same response to what today's religious enthusiasts would answer if we say that their god is just a symbol and not an actual god. Indians have a god for almost every environmental entity. Very similar to every mythology ever known. The gods are the personification of the natural observations unanswered. These are like gaps of knowledge filled with a temporary solution so that the larger message is not lost. Just a symbolism that we fail to accept even today for our own emotional dependence.

Vamana
(the Pygmy man)

The story

Once upon a time there was a king named mahabali. The grandson of Prahlad, who rose to power and conquered all three lokas namely 'Patal' - the underworld, 'Dharti' - the earthly world and swarga - the heavens. Vishnu in the form of Vamana, the dwarf avatar asked king mahabali to donate land taken by him in three steps, mahabali readily agreed as the dwarf nature of the avatar fooled the king of the distance he can travel in just 3 steps and agreed to it. Vamana took the first step in pataal, the second one on dharti and the third one in the sky. Reclaiming all the kingdom of mahabali, to restore normalcy by gifting all back to Indra.

Explanation

There is also another nature of the trilok given as earth, sky and heaven. So Vamana placed his first step on earth, the second in the sky and the third in heaven. Now there are many speculations already made to give meaning to the three steps of the avatar. Some say they symbolise the three states of nature: the earth, the sky and space. Some say it is the three steps of human consciousness namely the woken state, dream state and the deep sleep >18.

The avatar being dwarf in nature tells us the awareness of a different species of humans, homo floresiensis, whose remains were uncovered in Indonesia, or it could also be a reference to the pygmy people found in Africa. This story that Vamana avatar comes before the human avatar gives us indication of the knowledge of the awareness of not only the presence of another species but that those other species came into being before us.

Now an interesting fact is that the word pygmy comes from Greek literature. Homer, the ancient poet describes pygmy as a tribe of dwarfs, living in India >19. The same poet who wrote iliad, the story of trojan war, whose similarity to Ramayana has been a topic of debate since a long time.

Parshuram

(the first immortal)

The story

Once upon a time there lived a great sage named Jamadhagni. Jamadhagni is said to be the inventor of sandals, called paduka and umbrella. He had married Renuka, who was born in a Kshatriya family. Parshuram was their youngest son. Renuka had a divine pot that was made of unbaked clay. The pot was held together by the power of devotion of Renuka towards her husband. Once Gandharvas, the artists of heaven, were traveling in the sky. Renuka lost her devotion to her husband for a moment. The water in the pot that Renuka was carrying on her head fell and completely drenched her. She was afraid to face her husband in this state. She went to her friend, a fisherman's wife. Jamadhagni got enraged realising what had happened. He asked his eldest son to go and kill his mother for her momentary lapse of devotion. But the eldest son refused to carry out this inhumane task. Jamadhagni turned his son into a stone. All his sons refused to carry out the task and were turned into stone one by one. Rambhadra the youngest son could not refuse a task given by his father and accepts his father's inhumane order.

Jamadhagni was the son of Richika, a great sage and Satyavati, daughter of a king named Gaadhi. When Richika asked the king for his daughter's hand in marriage, the king asked the sage to bring a thousand horses. After the sage completes the task he wins Satyavati's hand in marriage. After the marriage Satyavati and her mother both ask the sage Richika for blessing for a child. Richika then prepared two meals of milk boiled rice. He gives the meal with Brahma mantra to his wife, so that a great sage will be born to Satyavati. He gives the meal with Kshatri mantra to his mother in law so that a great warrior will be born to her. Now Satyavati's mother decides to exchange their meals hoping that her son in law would have given a better blessing to his wife than mother in law. Satyavati, being young and naive, agrees to her mother's idea of the exchange. When Richika gets to know about this he informs them of the mantras and now states the fact that a great sage will be born to his mother in law and his wife shall bear a great warrior. His mother in law in time gives birth to a great sage called Vishwamitra. The grandson of Vishwamitra is the great king Bharat, after whom India was initially named as Bharat. Satyavati asks Richika for a way around this mantra. It was her wish that her child be a great sage. Richika says that the Kshatri mantra could be made to skip a generation. This would make the child of their son a great warrior.

Rambhadra had performed a great penance to lord Shiva and obtained an axe from the penances. By choosing to perform this most difficult task showed that he had inherited the mantra. Rambhadra then takes his weapon, the axe, and goes to kill his mother. He kills the fisherman and his wife who try to save his mother's life. Then Rambhadra also kills his mother and goes to report this to his father. Jamadhagni then asks Rambhadra for 2 gifts for performing the difficult task given by his father. Rambhadra asks the great sage to bring his mother back to life and to remove the stone curse on his brothers.

Rambhadra then goes on a pilgrimage. He raises the western coast of Bharat with the power of his great axe. In the meantime, Jamadhagni with his penances is able to get the great cow Surabhi, the daughter of Kamadhenu from heaven. Kartavirya Arjun, a great king of the time, wished to own the great cow. Jamadhagni refuses his wish but the king takes the cow by force. When Rambhadra gets to know about this he takes his axe and challenges the king to a battle. Rambhadra then kills the king in the battle and brings back the cow from the king. Jamadhagni then informs him that it is not the dharma or duty of a brahmin to kill a king. He then asks Rambhadra to perform penances for this sin. When Rambhadra returns from the penances he gets to know that the sons of the king killed Jamadhagni for revenge. The warrior clan of that time is said to have lost morality and were cruel. Rambhadra then challenges the sons and kills them in the battle. Rambhadra then receives several challenges from the warrior clans and kills them all in the challenges. Rambhadra in the 21 battles that happen kills all warrior races completely. Due to the great deeds performed by him only with the help of an axe he is titled as Parshuram.

Explanation

The weapon wielded by Parshuram is an axe. Axe in Sanskrit language is called Parshu. Hence he was given the title of Parshuram. The story where Parshuram is said to have raised the western shore of India with his axe is a symbolic one. Our school geography lesson came to answer again. We now know that the Himalayan mountains are fold mountains. The Indian landmass was once located near the equator than it is now. It slowly started to shift in a northeast direction 80 million years ago>20. Note the direction of the shift, Konkan or as the western coast of India is called, stretches from north east to south west. Perpendicular to the direction of movement. We can safely assume that this was the reason that the Konkan belt might have risen from the depths of the ocean. This could also answer the diversity of flora and fauna found in the region, being one of the most ecologically diverse in the world. Parshuram was also the first brahmin to wield a weapon. This symbolizes the start of an era of weapon research and development. No other culture gives you such a diverse variety of weapons as Indian culture. Parshuram could have been the one to start that research.

But the most important aspect of the man was that he unlocked immortality. Now immortality as a concept is a complex one. Indians mythology believes in 9 immortals. Every immortal gives us a form of immortality. This is just a wide categorization of what kind of people are always remembered. Hanuman is a devotee of lord Ram. Different cultures will give you different stories of people who were able to do impossible things due to their power of belief. Ashwathama is another example of an immortal, as he did a very heinous crime in the story of Mahabhartha. Today we have Hitler who is always given as an example of extreme cruelty. Now how is Parshuram immortal till today? He is still alive among his descendants. There is a separate sect of Brahmins who proclaim themselves as the descendants of Parshuram. This concept is used in the movie 'The Dark Knight returns'. Here the character of Ra's al Ghul haunts Batman even after his death which inspires Bruce to understand that the person tormenting him is a child of Ra's. In the comics the character is immortal having lived for more than 500 years. While rationalizing this concept of immortality Nolan, the writer and director of the movie gives us the answer to Parshuram's immortality.

The descendants of Parshuram successfully carried out inbreeding due to the social structure of India, where a girl is married into the groom's family. In the Chitpavan Brahmins girls were not allowed to marry outside the caste, but the women of other castes were allowed to marry into the family at least in the initial stage. This helped Parshurama to create a long lasting lineage, which is still alive and thriving. This made him immortal as his name is still carried forward by his living descendants.

To write this book I had to follow my instinct, sometimes thinking opposite to the currently accepted thoughts. I had to rely on my instinct to guide me in this path. Making my instincts my guru, I was able to decipher the knowledge hidden in this book and also, from this book.

Ram

(the ideal man)

The Story

Once upon a time in a jungle far away there lived a dacoit. He was feared by everyone. Mothers who were as far as 50 miles would say to their children to sleep or Valya the dacoit would come to take them away. He would loot the travelers in the jungle and mercilessly cut their index finger if they had no money. He wore a garland of the fingers around his neck with pride. Once a saint was traveling along that path. People had warned the saint of the dacoit but the saint said that he was a devotee of God and that God will save him in his travels. The dacoit saw the saint and stopped him in his tracks. The dacoit demanded money or a finger. The saint asked the dacoit why he was looting passengers? The dacoit said that he was doing it for his family. His parents, wife and children needed to be fed and they would die of hunger if he didn't do what he did. He cut their fingers so as to instill fear in their hearts. That fear made sure people gave their money and jewels instead of their fingers. The saint remained calm and asked him if he knew that he was committing dangerous sins and would be punished by God for these sins. He said he would do anything for his family. He added that he himself only wore the ornaments of the fingers and simple clothes. He didn't feel the need for great wealth, he did it all for his family. The saint thought that the dacoit was a simple misguided man who needed to be shown the true path. So calmly the saint said that he was a good man who was doing evil deeds, but is his family ready to share the sins as they shared the wealth? The dacoit answered that his family were an equal partner of him in his sins and was sure they would share the sins along with him. The saint asked him to confirm it with his family first, he said he would wait for his fate to be decided but wanted the dacoit to confirm this from his family members, for whom he did everything. The dacoit kept his men to watch the saint and went home to ask his family members. He first went to his parents, he told them that a saint had come and asked if they were willing to share his sins. His parents were shocked and flatly refused to take part in his sins. They said they had not raised him to be a dacoit and that the decision to be a dacoit was his own. The dacoit was flabbergasted. He thought that maybe his wife would support him. His wife said that she shared the burden of the family with him but the burden of his deeds was his and his alone. She says that it was his duty to be a provider to the family and how he did his part was his decision. The dacoit was now on the verge of losing his mind. But he looked at his children and as a last resort asked them if they shared the burden of his sins with him. His wife threw a tantrum after hearing this, she said her children will never suffer the sins of their father. She asked the dacoit what kind of a father he was, who wanted to make their children suffer the sins of his deeds, which they neither comprehend nor understand. The dacoit now completely lost it. He threw the garland of fingers that he wore around his neck and fell into the feet of the saint. He asked the saint for his forgiveness and accepted him as his disciple. The dacoit then went on to become the great saint called Valmiki.

Explanation

I have to start with a confession. There are parts in the story which I have added to make it more interesting. The part, which mentions the dacoit to be feared around 50 miles by mothers, is borrowed from a classic Indian movie, Sholay. Also there is a similar story of a dacoit called Angulimal (the one who wears a garland of fingers) who was guided by Buddha, which I have merged here. I took these artistic liberties intentionally for the people who are reading about the Ramayana with little to no knowledge. If they are unaware of the difference between these two stories, they could in time start believing that these were actually part of Valmiki's story in case I hadn't confessed. These small deviations don't change the original story, just add more features to it. In a similar way the stories of Ramayana received such small deviations throughout these years. These were a form of interpretation. Different people interpreted differently. The purpose of the deviations was also to add more features to it. The features made the stories more effective and highlighted the moral so that simple people would understand the complex aspects of the story as well. There are more than 300 interpretations of Ramayana >22.

Now the reason for me to do this is for us to understand the liberties taken by the writer of any story, as well as the people who further tell them. All the artists borrow ideas or inspiration from other art forms, nature and sometimes even true events. Now I believe that Valmiki is the creator of Ramayana. In many Indian sub cultures they say Valmiki constructed Ramayana, so Valmiki was the architect of Ramayana. Ramayana actually didn't happen but was created by Valmiki. If you believe that Ramayana actually happened I respect that and I expect you to at least consider my arguments and judge it individually.

Ramayana is a story of relations. It starts with Ravana, the antagonist of the story. It is a story of all kinds of relations. The only son dying in pursuit of his parents' wishes, Shravan mistakenly dies at the hands of king Dasharath, who himself invokes a curse from the parents that he too will die in longing for his children. A mother's affection for her child, Queen Kaikeyi persuades Dasharath, her husband, to send Ram, his eldest son and Kaikeyi's stepson in vanvas (to live a life of hermit) for 14 years so that her child Bharath can rule Ayodhya. A wife's dedication to her husband, Sita, who also accompanied Ram in vanvas, had to sacrifice the life of luxury and a wife's sacrifice for her husband, Urmila slept for 14 years on behalf of her husband Lakshmana, who stayed awake for 14 years. A brother's responsibility to accompany his brother in the difficult time, and to protect him and his wife, Lakshmana accompanied Ram and Sita in their vanvas to protect them in their long 14 years journey. A father's longing for his beloved sons, Dasharath, according to the curse of Shravan's parents, died longing to see his sons, especially Ram who was his eldest and favourite. A brother's feeling of protectivity for his sister who was disproportionately wronged for her mistakes. Ravana's sister Shurapanakha's nose was cut by Lakshmana for seducing his brother. A lover being friend zoned by his love, Sita after being kidnapped by Ravana, eventually started to like him but just as a friend. A brother mistakenly doubted his brother and threw him out of the family, Bali thought Sugriva betrayed him and threw his brother out of the kingdom. Rama was the assassin chosen by Bali to kill his brother Sugriva. Rama's price was Sugriva's help that he needed to rescue his wife. A brother's betrayal for being taken for granted and not getting the respect he deserves, Vibhishan betrayed Ravana and sided with Ram.

So why does Ramayana have so much emphasis on relations? It is because Valmiki had changed from Valya, a bandit to Valmiki, a sage due to his relatives not sharing his burden of sins. It had changed the man fundamentally. An artist uses art to express their feelings, hence the art reflects the artist's thoughts. A heartbroken person listens to sad songs that an artist created inspired from his own or sometimes other people's heartbreak. People who still believe that Ramayana actually took place will consider this as a weak argument. But people who believe that Ramayana happened uses the presence of Ayodhya city and ram setu connecting India and Sri Lanka as a proof of its actual happening. It is like believing in Harry Potter because of the presence of Kings cross station and then trying to access platform no 9 and 3/4. Today there is a board on the platform as a dedication to J K Rowling's famous creation. Say 500 years later someone believing in a world of wizards uses this board as a point of argument?

If we believe that Ramayana actually happened for the sake of argument even then the content of Ramayana is questionable. Who told Valmiki the complete story of Ramayana, all the minute details? We have to assume it was Sita, who is said to have lived in his ashram after Ram abandoned her in a pregnant state. Now the story of Shankar and Parvati is also a part of Ramayana. So the story was told to Ravana by someone, who then told it to Sita, who told it to Valmiki. And there were years of time in between the stories being told. So how can we say that there might have not been any kind of modifications. As in Ravana wouldn't have told the story of his failures to persuade Parvati to a woman he is still trying to persuade. And who told him the story of what happened after he left mount Kailasa, the story of Ganapati's head being replaced. The reason for the fabrication of the story of Ganapati will be discussed in more detail in the next avatars story.

Now if you still choose to believe that Ram actually lived then I would encourage you to do the same and follow your instincts. But make sure that if you believe that Ram truly lived then it should inspire you to follow in his footstep of self-sacrifice and not just have a shallow belief. Believe that Ram sacrificed his wife and children for the sake of the good of his kingdom and as a responsibility to his subjects. Just like Narendra Modi, a believer of Ram, sacrificed his marriage so as to be fully committed to hold a position of power. But also remember that Bhagat Singh, the great Indian freedom fighter, was a socialist and hence didn't believe in any god. He also refused to marry only to die for the freedom of his nation. Your belief in Ram or Bhagat

Singh doesn't make you better than the rest if you don't follow their path. I know how difficult it can be to follow in the footsteps of these great men. But considering them as supreme god makes it even more difficult. Consider them as your idols, your friends, companions. In Vedic times 12 names were given to Surya, the Sun god. The first name to be invoked is Mitraya, meaning a friend. Consider the holy energy as your friend first.

Nala Damayanti is a story of Rama's ancestors. The story is part of the Ramayana but the version we know of the story today is that which was written by Kalidasa, the great poet. The play written by Kalidasa is the story of Nala Damayanti told today. So this is exactly what happens when Harry Potter receives immense popularity, you get movies like Fantastic beasts and where to find them. A story based on the characters fleetingly mentioned in the original art.

The story that hanuman, the monkey god, carried the mountain Dronagiri in his hand is an example of taking things literally. Imagine a scenario where a wife asks husband to bring some goods from the supermarket. Husband forgetting the list told by the wife buys a couple of bags of goods more than what was asked, as the supermarket is about to close for the day. Wife not expecting the husband to bring in so many goods, jokingly asks if the husband bought the whole supermarket. A perfect example of exaggeration. Here replace husband by Hanuman and wife by Ram. Ram had asked Hanuman to bring in a specific plant. Hanuman had one chance to bring the Sanjeevani plant. He couldn't take any chance of missing that. Hence he might have carried several plants on a piece of mountain land which later got exaggerated to the whole mountain.

Another form of immortality is found in every culture worldwide. People following a faith tend to remember previous great followers, and their deeds done through the power of faith. That immortality is as a devotee. Hanuman was the biggest devotee of Ram. Hanuman along with Parshuram is one of the 8 immortals. His immortality lies in the form of his devotion. There are 3 philosophical paths of life according to Bharatiya culture. The 3 paths are knowledge, action and devotion. Knowledge is what scientists, seers and philosopher's walk on. Action is the path everyone walks on but the motivation and the direction of the action varies person to person. The last is the path of devotion, where every action you take is for the devotion of some human or faith. Hanuman is the best example for this path supporting Rama no matter what. Hanuman never questions Rama. His actions are all controlled by his devotion to Rama. One more reason to mention Hanuman is the 15th century poem dedicated to Hanuman, called Hanuman Chalisa. Hanuman chalisa mentions a line in which the distance of the sun from earth is discussed. These little pieces of knowledge hidden in a piece of art should encourage to find more hidden gems of knowledge of ancient Indian shlokas. There are many examples in Indian culture who gave in to the path of devotion. We find many saints and nuns in every culture whose stories of devotion are immortal.

Ravana, the villain is always characterized by his laughs but the name of Ravana actually means the one who cries. The root of the laughter of Ravana lies in the story where he composed and sang the shiv tandav stotra. Ravana tried to impress Parvati by lifting Mount Kailash. Shankar then pressed his foot to trap him under the mountain. Ravana then praised Shiva in his composition so that Shankar will release him from his prison. For his performance Shankar released Ravana and gifted him a sword named Chandrahas and a shivling.Now Shakespeare may have said what's in the name but in Indian culture if you want to understand the meaning of any concept all you have to do is study the name. There is even a belief in Indian culture where children are told to find the meaning of their life in their name. For example here the translation of the name of the sword means smile like a moon. A smile looks like a crescent moon. So if you are in any trouble, the best way to start would be to bring a smile to your face. Ravana as the name suggests was the one who cried hence it was after receiving this sword that he started to smile. The smile slowly turned into laughter until laughing loudly became his identity itself.

Shankar is originally just an avatar of Shiva. As Shiva is an energy of destruction of life just like Vishnu is an energy of conservation of life. Vishnu may have many avatars but in mythology there is only one avatar of Shiva. Hence slowly with time Shiva and Shankar fused into one singular entity. Again even Shankar is just a character in Ramayana.

Ramayana also has a very unique prop in it. The pushpaka vimana gives great pride to Indians. Believing that we used to possess the science of aeronautics but lost the knowledge with time. It is not completely untrue. A lot of the ancient Indian knowledge was lost when the universities of Takshashila, Nalanda and many other ancient universities were destroyed. Most of these ancient universities were founded during the Gupta period >23. Each of these universities had multiple libraries. Different libraries in the same university for different subjects. We can only imagine the vast treasure of knowledge lost. Now the Orville brothers built the first flying machine at the start of the twentieth century>24. But the great Leonardo da Vinci conceptualized it 5 centuries earlier >25. Both the aero plane and the helicopter were conceptualized by da Vinci. He studied the concept extensively and has famous drawings of those concepts. Now similarly we have found multiple concepts of flying machines in Indian literature. There were actually 4 types of vimana. The conceptualization of us flying in great machines was a great deal at that time. It was the belief that someday we can invent a device that will enable us to fly. It's like imagining interstellar travel today. We have already started conceptualizing practical interstellar travel. Both are groundbreaking concepts for their time. Maybe the way we actually do interstellar travel will be a lot different than how we are imagining now.

Krushna

(the perfect man)

The story

Once upon a time there lived a great man who had end to end knowledge of the Vedas due to which he was called Veda Vyas. One day he decided to write an epic story. The moral of the story was the summary of all the knowledge that he had gained from all the Vedas.

He had ink dyed from the indigo plant. His pages made from the papyrus tree were ready. He had a beautiful peacock feather that he used as a writing tool, just like a pen. He drank water first as he would not be able to drink water after sitting to write. The words written in indigo ink would be disillusioned if touched by water and his written work would be erased if water fell on the papyrus pages. After he started his task, he found that the speed of his thoughts was greater than the speed of his writing. This cut the flow of his thoughts and he was not able to continue writing. He then stopped writing and started to think for a way out of his predicament.

He thought that if someone else did the task of writing then he would find it easy to focus on the course of the story. At that time not many had the knowledge of the art of writing. Ganapati the leader of the region was the only person in the region who had the knowledge as well as practice of writing. As the leader of the people he communicated with the public from far and wide through writing scrolls. The crier then announced the scrolls to all the villages. Ganapati was the beloved leader of the people and would communicate frequently with them and was hence in practice of writing regularly. The criers had strict instructions of throwing the scrolls in water if a possibility of falling into the hands of the enemy arises. This made Ganapati ideal for the task Veda Vyas needed him for. He then asked Ganapati for his help. As Ganapati was the leader of the region, he was busy and declined the invitation. But Veda Vyas was unshakable in his pursuit. Finally Ganapati relented and accepted his invitation. But Ganapati made a condition that he should not be stopped once he started writing. Veda Vyas then added a condition of his own that Ganapati would have to understand each and every verse that he writes. They decided that they will not stop unless they complete the story. They then started their penance.

When Ganapati started writing, he did something unique. Something that not even the criers were aware of. Ganapati used to sometimes send out sensitive information to be delivered only to a specific person. At that time Ganapathi used to write with invisible ink, water. The crier would give the scroll to the concerned party. The message could be read only if held in light. Similarly Ganapathi wrote "om namah shivay" on every page where the earlier water did not percolate.

A whole day passed and night time arrived and Veda Vyas lit a wooden torch. Veda Vyas used to stop in between and ask questions to Ganapati to see if he understood the verses completely or not. Ganapati was otherwise writing continuously. Veda Vyas on the second day noticed that the temperature of Ganapati was rising due to the stress of the job and not being able to consume food or water. Veda Vyas started applying the nearby soil to Ganapati's body so as to cool him down. Their location was near a river and the soft clay like soil was ideal as it was what the potters used to make pots. These pots had the property to cool the water it held. Veda Vyas then placed pieces of banana leaves around his ears, so that soil will not enter his ears and placed a piece of long hollow vine on his nose and mouth, so that he could breathe comfortably. Ganapati kept water in his mouth to stay awake all the time. Applying soil on the forehead would affect his vision. So, Veda Vyas refrained from doing that. It looked as if the head of Ganapati was cut and replaced with the head of an elephant.

Both of them lost the sense of time while doing the task. After 10 days they finally completed the whole epic. But the situation of Ganapati was very critical. He had not consumed food for 10 days. Both of them had not slept for 10 days. But more critical was the condition of his outer body. The soil had got dry and removing it was going to be tricky. Tools could not be used as there was a chance that it might cut Ganapati. Veda Vyas carried Ganapati and immersed him in the nearby water stream. It was chaturdashi, the 14th day in the month of Bhadrapada. Shravan rains had bought enough water for the stream to be flowing with some speed. Veda Vyas dipped him once the soil on the body that had gone dry got moist. The second time most of the soil washed away. Third dip was enough to wash all the soil away. Coming out Ganapati was famished and asked Veda Vyas for lots of modaks as they were his favorite sweet and as a celebration for their achievement. Veda Vyas decided to aptly name the epic as Jaya.

Explanation

Now Ramayana can be debated if it really happened or not but not Mahabharata, as the epic Jaya is known today as. People still like to argue that Veda Vyas was writing what happened in the past and he was just a chronicler of what happened. But in that case he would not have needed the help of Ganapati to write. He needed the help because he was not writing from memory but writing from his imagination. The story formed faster in Veda Vyas's head but he was not able to write it at the same speed. If Veda Vyas was writing from his memory he would not have been in this predicament and would have been able to write Jaya without Ganapati's help. We should also be able to conclude the story of Ganapati in Ramayana was fabricated at some point of time. Ganapathi was a new god that was to be revered from at some point of time. So how do you introduce a new god and make sure people don't forget the fact that he is a god. Hence people were told to pray to Ganapathi first, before starting a new task. This was conveyed as a command from his father the great God Shankara aka Shiv himself so that no one questions the idea why Ganapati should be worshipped. This is why ganapati started being worshipped first. The earliest reference of Ganapathi or Ganesha as a god starts from the 1st century CE. It's highly possible that Ganesha the son of Parvati later takes the post of a Ganapati in the story. Ganapati was a position held in the society by the leader of the people. People who did this had no bad intentions. They must have felt like parents, parents who fool the people for their own good so that they develop healthy habits in their lives. Most of the older temples in India are located on the top of a hill. The long walk to the temple is itself an intense physical exercise. The feeling of reaching the top gives us an intense mental sense of achievement.

But I am sure some people will still believe that Mahabharata still actually happened. Well I will say again the same thing: follow your own instinct but do not hesitate to ask questions that arise in your mind. Always remember the laws of nature cannot be broken. People like to believe in magicians or other performers performing feats that defy science and logic but they use a combination of the art of deception and tricks to do those tasks. The tricks have to be kept a secret, if the secret is opened the people will lose interest and forget about it.

Now there is only one version of Mahabharata unlike Ramayana as the story was written down originally. It stunted any growth of fabrications but it was not able to stop the fabrications completely. The best way to spot a fabrication is to identify something that's unnatural. Like the story Krishna holding up mount Govardhan on his little finger to save his village people from torrential rains. Now the story tells that Krishna asked the people of his village to stop praying and performing any rituals to lord Indra, the king of heavens and the god of rains. The rituals were just a remnant of their occupation of agriculture before they became herders. Indra was also the most beloved god of that time. The most invoked god in Vedas is Indra. Krishna asked his people to worship mount Govardhan as it was where their herds grazed and was a more apt symbol to be worshipped.

But the elders of the village opposed him. Coincidentally the heavens opened and it started to rain heavily. Now the story says that Krishna lifts Mount Govardhan completely on the small finger of his left hand to accommodate all the villagers under it. Now Vrindavan where the story happens is located near the banks of Yamuna River. In the times of heavy rains would it be wise to remain on base of the mountain where the river water could easily reach in case of floods? As per the story it rained continuously for 7 days. The river would have definitely had floods. So instead of lifting the mountain the natural response would have been to climb on it. It does not change the narrative of the story one bit. After all the people had safely gathered on the top of the mountain, the village elders started blaming Krishna for vexing lord Indra and bringing his wrath in the form of rains. Krishna then mentioned his observation that what happens proves that mount Govardhan is more worship worthy as it has saved them from the wrath of Indra.

Now the currently accepted location of Govardhan mountain is 25 kms from the currently accepted location of Vrindavan, and almost the same distance from Gokul, another place where Krishna grew up. Vrindavan is closer to Mathura, where king Kansa ruled who wanted Krishna dead, than to Govardhan mountain. It takes roughly around 5 hours to walk from Mathura to Govardhan mountain. And that's straight walking, animals don't walk straight and it would take a lot more time to walk if you are herding animals. But still we will stick to the 5 hour time. Is it possible to walk

10 hours daily so that herds would graze for a mere 3 hours? As they would have to be back to Vrindavan before the day ends or else they could lose the animals in the dark. This proves that at some time in the past people assigned these places and may have been an imaginary place in the story. This helps us understand how the stories and their current location are fabricated. Krishna is a known rationalist. He propagated the theory of Karma not bhakti. Your deeds are the way you communicate with god. The holy spirit doesn't have ears to hear you or eyes to see you. The only way you can communicate to God is through your work. The story of the menacing form of Krishna is described during his famous discussion with Arjuna, the meaning of that menacing form will be explained in the last Avatar. If you carefully read the Vedas, The god most invoked in Vedas is Indra. The word Indra is similar to Indriya which means senses. So the symbol of the king of heaven is your own senses. Meaning you will experience heaven on earth if you stay in your senses. Indra was the chief god at that time meaning it was a subtle way reminding people to stay in their senses.

There are many more gems of knowledge hidden inside Mahabharata. Karna was the 1st born son of Kunti. But Kunti had him when she was young and unmarried. Karna is said to have been born with a gold chest plate and earrings. Karna was the son of Kunti and the sun. Now it is not scientifically possible that the sun himself is the father of Karna, but it's a very beautiful concept. The child obtained it from a man who charmed the girl. So the other five children should give some hints relating to their fathers hidden in the symbolism. Now another idea is that Kunti gave those gold ornaments to Karna. She was the princess of a kingdom. When she understood that there is no other option than to part with her first born, she wanted to make sure someone took care of him and also find a way to identify the boy in the future. But a child weighs an average of 3.5 kg. The armor should have been as thin as possible. It must have been carved with the sun emblem. Now the armor didn't grow naturally as Karna did. It had to be expanded little by little as he was growing up. Gold has a property that it can be beaten into very thin sheets without it breaking. Thinner than any other natural metal. This property in today's science is called malleability. So thin that you can even eat it. This might be a common knowledge today but Indians knew this property about gold even before Mahabharata was written. Just one of the several gems of knowledge that were hidden in Jaya. Now I don't believe the story was tampered intentionally at any time. Karna, when left by Kunti, was fortunately found by a childless couple, who took care of him like their own son. The couple found Karna in that state and the simple minded couple might have truly believed that he was a god sent child. We started believing that Karna was naturally born with it because that's what his adopted parents told people in the story. Also the part that the gold was stuck to Karna's body could have been what the adoptive parents told people so that no one tries to steal the gold from the boy.

Mahabharata can be directly compared to one modern day epic, a song of fire and ice, commonly known as game of thrones. The comparison can be made in more than one way. It is because the story of game of thrones itself is inspired from the war of roses. An event that happened around 550 years ago. Game of thrones also had an addition of supernatural content to make things more interesting. Similarly there was a kuru empire that ruled around 8 - 9 century BCE, which might have been an inspiration for the great epic Jaya. Mahabharata started being compiled around the 4th century BCE and reached its final form in the 4th century CE, which was the early Gupta period. Jaya was written in one sitting in a span of 10 days but it took 8 centuries to turn it into Mahabharata >26.

The reason Jaya had to be changed again can be found in the name. Jaya means victory. In the war of Mahabharata Krishna asked Pandavas to break many laws of war sometimes even against their own will. He was a propagator of Karma. Now people started getting inspired and were ready to break any laws for victory. Lawlessness might have crept in the society slowly. To stop this lawlessness and bring back some modicum of stability was the reason for the change of Jaya to Mahabharata, it was not done with any wrong intention. Asoka himself had killed his brothers for the throne of Magadha. After accepting Budhha as his guru he had to make sure that no other brother made the same mistakes he did.

Jaya was the biggest work of literature ever created. It contains 1.8 million words. For comparison the closest single work of literature with 1.7 million words is the song of fire and ice series. And with the upcoming winds of winter and dream of springs the 2.5 millennia old record of Jaya can finally be broken. It took George R

R Martin more than 3 decades to write what Veda Vyas and Ganapati wrote in 10 days. It is possible only because of the nature of Sanskrit language.

How were the changes made to the great epics like Mahabharata and Ramayana? It is very easy to imagine it in today's time. Game of Thrones is the name of just the first book of the series but we remember it because of the series. We now know the story without actually reading the books. Similarly in those times plays could have been performed from the stories of Ramayana and Mahabharata. Even today it's a tradition of watching Ramleela during the Navratri festival. But there are always some changes done while translating books into visual art form. Some artistic liberties are taken and people start identifying the liberties taken as part of the original stories. Example today Sherlock Holmes is characterized by his famous deerstalker hat. It was just worn once in the entire Sherlock Holmes literature. But was made famous by a stage actor. Even the story track of the game of thrones series and book is vastly different. And we all know which is the story that we will remember.

The weapon of choice for Krishna was sudarshan chakra. The name sudarshan literally translates to "good vision". "Su " is a suffix added before any word for saying good. So sudarshan chakra literally means the cycle of good vision. Krishna always used to see good in others, it's what made him liked by everyone. People who always say good things are liked by everyone. But that does mean they have to be lying or at least ignore the truth sometimes. This is the reason they say that it was the children of Krishna that bought the Kaliyuga. This just symbolizes that the truth is hidden in this time period. The ultimate truth that we will study in the last Avatar. When you lie you have to believe that lie first. Only then can you convince others that you are not lying. Now you are the first person to hear what you say, you never notice that because you do that subconsciously. Also now you have to remember the lie as well as the truth. This adds a very little tension to your brain. Now to hide that one lie we have to lie some more times. Now you really start to feel that tension in your mind. Because you have to remember to whom you have lied, what you have lied, why you have lied and the truth as well. So with this you are increasing the pressure on your brain with basically useless information. Mind palace is a widely accepted concept for a strong memory. It is also fleetingly mentioned in the original Sherlock literature. In this concept you keep all the useful information you possess systematically. This can happen only if no junk and useless information is stored in the brain. This is only a way of optimizing your brain memory power. So by always speaking the truth you are able to keep your mind palace as well as your brain performance at its optimum. This is the power of the truth.

Mahabharata gives us another example of immortality. The teacher of Kauravas and Pandavas was Dronacharya. Dronacharya had a son named Ashwatthama. The father and the son duo were fighting for Kauravas against the protagonist Pandavas. During the battle Dronacharya was being difficult to take down and his battles were helping Kauravas greatly. Dronacharya was fighting alone but no one was able to take him down. Instead of taking on Dronacharya in the battlefield, which until that point was not producing any results in the war. Krishna asked Bheema, the second Pandava, to kill an elephant. Bheema then started shouting that he had killed Ashwatthama. Dronacharya initially thought there must be some mischief. Krishna was famous for that since he was a toddler. It didn't help being deep in the enemy camp. He was not able to concentrate in the battles. Dronacharya decided to ask the only person he trusted in the Pandava clan, the Eldest Pandava, Yudhisthira. Yudhisthira was also named Dharma due to his commitment to follow the dharma or the law. Dharma meaning the ideal way of life did not allow lying in any case. When Dronacharya asked Yudhishthira if his son was killed in that day's battle or not. Yudhisthira replied that Ashwatthama was killed today and then Krishna's idea muttered softly that it was a man or an elephant. Dronacharya lets his arms down and immediately gets taken down by Arjuna. After the great battle of Mahabharata Ashwatthama kills all the remaining sons and some grandsons of Pandavas. He performed these cruel acts when the young ones were in their sleep and after the great war was over. This act was just the frustration of Ashwatthama releasing due to the way the rules of war were broken, bent and manipulated by Pandavas especially Krishna in the name of victory or as the name of the original title suggests Jaya. Ashwatthama was cursed to live forever due to this act. It is comparable to the holocaust of World War 2. The cruelty of Hitler has made his name to be remembered for generations as an example that should not be followed, in a way similar to Ashwatthama.

Buddha

(the peace bringer)

The story

The chariot was passing through the forest in Lumbini. The charioteer was riding as safely as possible. The queen of Kapilvastu, Maya, was in the chariot. Carrying her son in her womb. She stopped the chariot in a beautiful grove just near Lumbini. Lumbini was her father's place. It was the full moon night in the month of Vaishakh. Suddenly she started having labor pains. She gave birth to a handsome boy. The king of Shakhas, Suddhodana and the father of the boy, immediately brought his son and wife back to the capital. Sage Asita, the royal teacher, came to see the baby. The sage saw the child and asked the mother if she had seen an elephant in her dreams. The startled queen told the sage her dream of a white elephant with 8 tusks. She had the dream before she was even carrying the boy. Sage Asita predicted that the child will be a great saint or a great king. Queen Maya died within a week of the birth of the boy. Sage Asita deduced it could have been due to the birth of the child in the jungle. Young Siddhartha needed additional care. He was taken care of by his mother's sister, Prajapati. She was later married to the king. Suddhodana wanted Siddhartha to be a great king hence he decided to hide the full prophecy and tell Siddhartha only half of the prophecy.

Years rolled by Siddhartha grew into a young boy. He had already started showing signs of compassion. One day while Siddhartha was playing in the gardens he saw a bird falling to the ground. The bird was knocked by an arrow. Siddhartha took the bird and started to tend it's wound. Suddenly someone came running triumphantly. It was Devdutta, a cousin of Siddhartha. He started asking Siddhartha to give the bird. Siddhartha refused but Devdutta was not letting it go. Soon the quarrel turned up in the king's court. The king, intending to be unbiased towards his son asked Siddhartha what right did he have on the bird? Siddhartha calmly replied that he was not willing to give the bird to Devdutta. Devdutta argued that he had knocked the bird and hence it was his right to the bird. Siddhartha replied to Devdutta that the right of ownership should belong to the person who had saved the life of the bird and not the one who knocked it down. The royal court agreed to Siddhartha's arguments and praised his level of understanding and compassion. The whole court was satisfied that day seeing the compassion of Siddhartha but Suddhodana was worried. He could see his son going on the path of a great saint. From that day on the king started keeping Siddhartha occupied in various weapon training and grooming Siddhartha to be a great king. The king cut off Siddhartha from the world. He was rarely allowed to leave the royal palace. But Siddhartha's story of compassion for the bird could not be caged.

Years rolled by and Siddhartha turned into a fine young man. Suppabuddha, father of Devdutta, had a daughter named Yashodhara. He decided to perform her marriage. He arranged for her Swayamvar. This was a ritual in which a girl was shown various suitors and asked to choose her partner from the suitors. Yashodhara, hearing of his great compassion, chose Siddhartha. This angered Devdutta. He asked questions on the capability of Siddhartha. Usually, a Swayam Var used to be preceded with a competition. Devdutta conveyed to his father, a big noble man of the land, that Yashodhara was choosing a sinking ship. He forced his father to hold a competition of different weapons and then ask Yashodhara to choose her husband. Siddhartha, to the dismay of Devdutta, became victorious in all the competitions. Yashodhara married Siddhartha.

Siddhartha was living a life of fulfillment and happiness. Suddhodana finally gave into the long denied request of Siddhartha to go beyond the royal palace. Siddhartha was excited to finally go out. Suddhodana instructed his charioteer, Channa, to take his son for a ride in his kingdom. The subjects were seeing their prince for the first time. All of them were praising Siddhartha for his beauty. Siddhartha liked the feeling of being loved by his subjects. They came across an old man. Siddhartha saw the peculiar features of old age like wrinkled skin and weak body for the first time. Further ahead they saw a sick man crying in pain. Siddhartha's heart went out for the person and asked Channa to stop the chariot but Channa rode on saying it could be contagious. When Siddhartha met with his subjects, everyone was glad to meet him. Everyone was being friendly with him. Slowly they started to express their griefs and troubles to the prince. Siddhartha wanted to help everyone. Now he was feeling very restless. Seeing the suffering of his subjects had moved him to the core. He asked Channa to take him back home. Coming back home they saw a saint in meditation. Siddhartha felt a little calm seeing the saint. He was going to talk to the saint when Channa stopped him saying that saints shouldn't be disturbed when in meditation. Siddhartha was drawn to the calmness of the saint. Channa also told him of the prophecy made by sage Asita. Sage Asita had predicted he would be a great king like his father told him or a great saint. This made Siddhartha even more restless. Even after returning to his palace, to his Yashodhara all he could think of was the sadness he found in the people. He wanted to find the truth and the root of sadness.

Yashodhara, who was carrying his child, gave birth to a boy. But even the birth of his child didn't bring peace to Siddhartha's mind. He was still feeling restless. On the seventh night after the birth of his son, Siddhartha decided to leave his royal life and become a mendicant. He knew his family would take care of both mother and child. He knew he had to walk this path alone. He called Channa and told him to get horses ready for a midnight stroll. After wandering for some time in the southern direction of the palace. He got down from the horse and told Channa to go back. Channa looked at his gold ornaments. Siddhartha smiled and mumbled "almost forgot". He removed his ornaments and Channa leaves. He started walking. He couldn't understand where he was going. He just started walking south. He just kept walking. He felt tired and slept in the nearby ditch some distance from the road. He knew his father would try to find him and bring him back.

He woke up the next day. He felt hungry and started walking. He found another hungry man begging him for food. He informed the man he too was hungry and had nothing to eat. The hungry man looked at him but he didn't believe it. He took a look at him and guessed that Siddhartha belonged to a royal family. Siddhartha was stunned. The man asked Siddhartha his name, Siddhartha calmly replied "Gautama". He told the man that he would trade clothes with him if he could help him eat something. The hungry man looked at Siddhartha's clothes and agreed immediately for the deal. He took him to a nearby banana grove. While eating the man spoke about a village walking distance of half a day to the west. He took some bananas with him and started to walk. When he came to the village he asked a barber if he could cut his hair for some bananas. He started walking towards the city of Rajagriha, the capital of Magadha kingdom. He felt drawn to the city. The city was blessed with great Tirthankar like Mahavir and had various schools of thinking. He started begging for food and spent every waking moment thinking about finding the root of sorrow and unhappiness.

He listened to different schools of thoughts for years. Followed different methods taught by these schools. But no school of thought had the answer to his question. The tradition of Vipassana in the Buddhist school of thought helped to calm his mind. The Buddhist teachers would say that maybe his answers will be answered by the next Buddha. There had been Buddha's before who had guided humanity through their teachings. One day Bimbisara, the king of Magadha, saw him begging for food. Bimbisara went to meet him. Bimbisara was a kind hearted king. He went to Siddhartha, introduced himself and exchanged names. He said "Gautama, you look like you are from a royal family. If hard times have fallen on you let me give you a job in my court".

Siddhartha calmly rejected his offer. He informed Bimbasara he was looking for the root of sadness and unhappiness. Bimbisara was elated to know that. He told Siddhartha to come to him if he finds his answers.

Siddhartha then traveled looking for solace and peace. He found it in the jungles of Urubilva, near the modern day city of Gaya. Siddhartha then started growing more frustrated every day. He decided to punish himself for not being able to find answers. He started to starve himself. Eating meagre portions of food. He became weak. One day after taking his bath in the river, he started walking towards his meditation place. He suddenly felt weak and fell on the ground. With great effort he was able to walk to his meditation place. Next day, the daughter of the nearby herdsman gave some food to Siddhartha. He found that starving himself was not going to help him find his answers. He decided to follow a healthy diet. One day he decided that he will not leave his meditation until he finds the answers to his question. He sat for a long time. The clouds of a storm started gathering in the sky. It slowly started to drizzle. Soon it became a full blown rainstorm. But Siddhartha decided to battle through it and not to leave meditation. He found it difficult to meditate. His mind was desiring comfort in that storm. Suddenly a thought ran across Siddhartha's mind. Desire is the root of all evil. But Siddhartha was still not sure if the answer was right or wrong. He thought of God and said " hey god tell me if I am right or wrong ". He felt the storm receding. He opened his eyes and saw the sun shining upon him and the clouds of storm slowly thinning out. Siddhartha saw the land illuminating just like his mind was illuminating with knowledge.

Slowly and steadily Buddha started gaining followers. He preached dhamma, to sit in meditation and sangha, to gather people together. Hundreds of people sat in vipassana under his guidance. People found peace and solace in his methods and words. Bimbisara heard about him and invited Siddhartha to Rajagriha and arranged for his sermons. After hearing his sermons he too like many others found Buddha, the great teacher everyone was waiting for. He gave the Venu forests in his kingdom to Buddha and his followers. Buddha started teaching his sermons there. Many people went to Buddha to find answers to their sufferings and found the peace in his knowledge. One day a woman came weeping to Buddha. Her child had died in infancy and she was distraught. All she kept asking from Buddha was to bring her child back to life. She was not ready to listen to anything else. Buddha promised her he will bring the child back to life but he needed an ingredient that is hard to find, if she is able to give him that ingredient only then could he bring her child back to life. He asked to bring him a few mustard seeds from a house where death had not taken place. The grieving woman went from door to door but found no home without a home. After tiring down from the exercise, she went to Buddha and became his disciple. His teachings started gaining fame far and wide. One day Suddhodana on hearing about him invited him to Kapilvastu.

He accepted his offer and came to Kapilvastu with his followers. The king arranged for a grand feast where everyone in the city was present. Buddha talked and answered everyone's question calmly. He suddenly noticed the absence of Yashodhara. A teenage boy came to Buddha and touched his feet to gain blessings. Buddha felt drawn towards the boy and picked him up. The boy told Buddha that he was his son Rahula and his mother had sent him to ask for his share of family belongings. Buddha smiled and said his only belonging was his knowledge. And he would be more than happy to share it with his son. Buddha took Rahula as his disciple and went to meet Yashodhara. Yashodhara had earlier refused to go and meet Buddha as she was restless and distraught for years due to him. He had left without saying anything to anyone. In the early people made fun of her for it. With no news of him, years of rumours of his second marriage went flying around. Finally after years Buddha was able to calm her mind. His words brought peace to her heart. After learning that Rahula had joined the sangha she too became his disciple too. Many of the members of the royal family became his disciples. One of them was Devdutta. Along with his sister he had become a butt of jokes due to Siddhartha. He believed that Siddhartha was faking it all for publicity. Now suddenly the people were following his brother in law. He thought that it was due time for Siddhartha to retire to his family and sister and volunteered to lead Sangha. Buddha kindly declined his offer and said his work was far from over. Devdutta took the rejection to his heart and started plotting for Buddha's downfall.

He traveled to Rajgirha and met Ajatsatru, the son of Bimbisara. Ajatsatru was an ambitious king and felt his father's generosity was hampering the growth of the kingdom. He had started getting restless for power. Devdutta met Ajatshatru and helped him kill Bimbisara and Ajatshatru became king. Devdutta asked for Ajatsatru's help to kill Buddha. Ajatsatru had invented a weapon that threw huge boulders. But Buddha escaped their well laid plan. A few of Devdutta's followers, who he had sent to kill Buddha, even started following him. This angered Devdutta. He asked Ajatsatru to send the royal elephant Nilgiri on Buddha's path in an inebriated state. Nilgiri was given buckets of alcohol to drink and sent in the path of Buddha. But Buddha still emerged unharmed. Ajatsatru slowly with time started losing his empire and with it his peace of mind. He decided to meet Buddha. He went to the famous mango grooves, called Amrapali, where Buddha was preaching. He found out that Buddha had thousands of followers at Amrapali at that time. When he reached Amrapali he found the place to be so silent that he believed the numbers he had heard were exaggerated. Walking a few steps he was stunned to silence. He saw Buddha sitting in the centre of more than a thousand people all meditating in a silent vipassana state. He felt a strong emotion of guilt and decided to become a disciple of Buddha. Devdutta realised his mistakes after a few years and decided to meet Buddha but died on the way to meet him. Buddha lived a long life teaching his methods and knowledge.

Explanation

Buddha was not the only saint to have come from India. India has been blessed with many great thinkers since ancient times till modern day. Mahavir came and preached just some 100 year before Buddha. The teachings of Buddha spread far and wide under Asoka's rule a couple of centuries later. Different sub cultures in the vastly diverse land of India project different nominees for this avatar. There are different parts in India who believe a local deity to be the 9th avatar of Vishnu. It is the only avatar who is challenged for his position. But Vipassana as a state of mind is a method every human being should experience. The stories of the previous lives of Buddha are collected together as Jataka tales. Just like Aesop's fables they are famous for their morals and short story length. Many Buddhist believe in the previous lives of Buddha. There are many stories of Buddhas who preceded Siddhartha.

Indian culture dictates that time is an endless cycle. The end of a period of time is just the start of a new period of time. Just like the end of a year starts a new year, similarly the end of a great period of time or an era starts a new period of time. Indian culture divided life into 4 yugas or eras. The 1st is Satya Yuga which encompasses the 1st 4 avatars namely matsya, kurma, varaha and narasimha. Notice that the rise of humans in the Avatar chronology coincides with the end of Satya Yuga. Basically, a symbol that lying is an inherent part of human psychology. The next 3 avatars Vamana, Parshuram and Ram came in treta yuga. The next avatar of Krishna came in Dwapar yuga. And Buddha and Kalki, the last Avatar Kalki will bring the end of Kaliyuga.

Now if these divisions of time had been made by God they would be the same for all humans just like the laws of science are the same for all. So these were not made by God but created by great minds for a simpler understanding of the cycle of nature. But inherently created by man. So Vishnu who is a supreme god and preserver of the whole universe took all the 9 avatars in the kingdom of Bharat and presumably the 10th Avatar will also be a Bharatiya. Isn't Vishnu being a little biased towards Bharat. The supreme lord preserver was biased toward this holy land and yet it was still under the rule of different foriegn invaders for the last 1500 years. Understanding that it's all just a symbolism is very important. Just like Budhha who has led many followers over the years. Moses, Jesus, Mohammed, Guru Nanak and countless other great men have gained followers for their great thoughts and compassion. In a similar way they all deserve to be Avatars of Vishnu. Some of the above mentioned great men have gained even more followers than Buddha. So why is Buddha still considered to be greater avatars of Vishnu to be included in the Dashavatar? Apart from Moses who was born a millennia before Buddha, most of the men mentioned above were born after the Dashavatars were compiled. The knowledge held by the great men who compiled these Avatars was only limited to Bharat. Hence all these avatars have stories embedded in this region of land. But as we have already understood, the knowledge held by the stories is beyond all borders of land and culture.

Kalaki

(The last man standing)

The story

Once upon a time 5 blind men came across an elephant. Each blind man contacted the elephant at different parts of its body. One blind man was touching the trunk of the elephant. Other one was touching the animal's stomach. The ear was held by one of them and the tusk by another. The final blind man had the tail in his hands. The blind men started singing praises of the animal they had encountered. When they listened to the characteristics mentioned in the praise of other blind men they found that the other blind men were wrong. Slowly they started fighting amongst each other about which of them was right.

Description

An avatar of God that has yet to come. A ray of both, hope and despair. The Avatar of God that will bring an end to time. The story mentioned above has nothing to do with the story of Kalki but an important key for the understanding of this Avtar. We have to study different cultures and science together in order to achieve the next step of our evolution.

The technological revolution is at the centre of the philosophical aspect of the end of time. Today due to the modern computers and internet an age-old philosophy of India ``Vasudhaiva Kutumbakam " (All the earthlings are one family) comes true. Smartphones brought this technology in the palm of our hands. Today we are living so co-dependent on each other that it would not be unfair to call the earthlings finally living as a family. Humans are slowly warming up to the fact that humanity transcends deeper than nation, culture, race and even religion. The scientific study and the technological development since the birth of humans has now progressed us to this stage. It's not like the connection was absent before smartphones. Telegram and Telephone laid the groundwork in the initial phase of the communication revolution. The Internet was developed for altogether different reasons than what we use today. Today it's irreplaceable in almost every commercial, professional and even personal aspect of our lives. The importance of smart phones lies in our personal connectivity through the internet. The rise of smartphones connected all of us on a more personal basis. Online platforms like gaming, social media connect people from all around the globe. This connection transcends all of our differences. Today, for the first time in the history of man, we are truly living as a citizen of the earth.

The rise of humanity is best described as exponential. Our Universe is believed to be around 14 billion years old. Our solar system is around 8-9 billion years old. Our earth is almost 4 billion years old. And humans are rumoured to be just 400,000 years old. In the history of this universe, we humans are still babies. In 2012 humanity was born in the

most physical sense as science requires it to be. Imagine a human, a bird and a butterfly. 3 different processes of birthing in nature. Humans like all other mammals carry their newly born in the womb of their females. A female bird lays an egg for the purposes of reproduction. A butterfly is born from a caterpillar. A human child in the womb is in the process of birthing.

It is still not yet fully born but is still alive. The different parts of the body are developed slowly and steadily. The child born is the collection of the different parts developed individually in the mother's womb. Similar process happens in an egg. A caterpillar goes into a cocoon for some time before changing its form and getting reborn as a butterfly. We are born in the egg of this solar system. The symbol of zero symbolizes an egg. The stage before 1 unit of animal is that particular animal's egg. The symbol inspired from nature is very similar to an egg, which is what comes before that 1 animal is hatched. The planets orbit the sun in the shape of an egg. The sun represents the yolk of the egg. Humanity started hatching out of this egg thanks to the Voyager 1 and 2 spacecrafts. Voyager 1 broke into interstellar space on 25th August 2012. And Voyager 2 on 5th November 2018. When a bird comes out of the egg its first successful attempt at breaking out of its shell is considered the start of the birthing process. Similarly, we humans broke out of our shell of the solar system in 2012. This symbolizes the end of time. Hence, we can say that in this way the Mayan prophecy of the end of time came true. It is the end of a Yuga, a long period of time. Today we are truly living in the time of the future, where knowledge and truth are easily accessible via the internet.

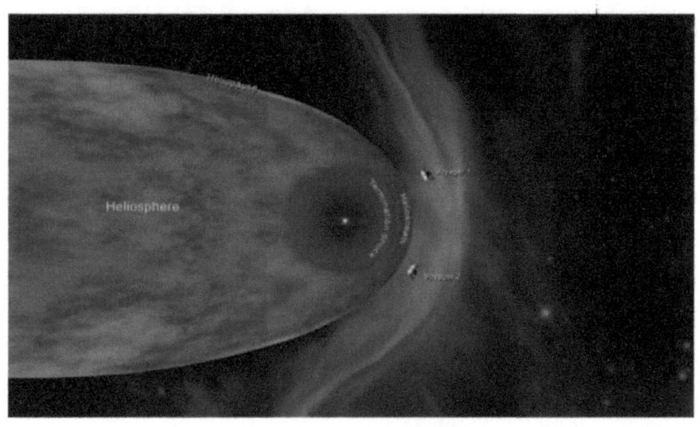

Kardashev made a scale that measures the reach of a civilization. The measure is based on the consumption of energy. In the first stage of civilization, it will be able to extract all the energy of its planet. In the second stage a civilization extracts all the energy of its solar system. In the third stage it will be able to completely harvest the energy of its galaxy. Today we are still a type zero civilization. In 2012 we had reached a level of 0.72 on the Kardashev scale. It was the physical sense of evolution. When an animal breaks its egg it takes some time to hatch. Even our first two taps on the egg were 6 years apart. Scientists believe that it would take us 100-200 years to reach the 1st stage of the Kardashev scale. Around 11,000 years to reach type 2. And possibly stage 3 in 100,000 to 1,000,000 years. Now it is also a possibility that we will be able to extract energy on Mars sooner than we are able to extract all the energy that can be generated on earth. So we will possibly start our journey towards stage two of the Kardashev scale even before completing stage 1. This indicates the stages overlapping each other. We are already working out on paths to complete the stage 2 stage of civilization. Ideas like Dyson sphere or using stellar engines to move the son have already been theorized. If the idea of a stellar engine is successful, we can travel around in the milky way carrying out the solar system similar to how a tortoise or turtle carries their shell. So if in the first stage of Kardashev scale we are able to hatch from an egg like a fish, the first Avatar. The 2nd stage is like a tortoise or a turtle, the 2nd avatar, carrying our shell of the solar system along with us. The cycle of evolution that has evolved us from millions of years before could be what guide us in the future as well. Similarly when we reach the third level on the Kardashev scale, our focus would be to hunt other galaxies as well for their resources. Hence the 3rd type in Kardashev is similar to the third avatar of a boar, which symbolizes hunting for survival.

Kalki Avatar is closely linked with destruction. Some interpret it as the destruction of ignorance and an untruthful mentality. Some say that humans would have forgotten humanity and will be eating each other, so Kalki will kill all humans and be the last man standing. These were interpretations made by great philosophers of yesteryear. Still it leaves us on a cliffhanger about what exactly to expect from the avatar. Another question arises as to why was the aspect of destruction given so much emphasis in Kalki's story? For that particular we have to go see the god of destruction, Shiva. The symbol of Shiva is the Shivalinga. Now we will understand the meaning of Shivlinga in 2 ways. One by its physical form and the second by its name. In the verb form the word shiva means "touch". The word Linga means our genitals. Hence even the word Shivalinga means touching of the genitals. Now the Shivalinga in the physical form looks like this. A conjugation of the male and the female genitals.

Now after learning the meaning of Shivalinga many a Hindus feel ashamed and straight away deny or refuse to accept it in its true form. They say after the Kali Yuga the age of darkness the Satya Yuga will rise again. Basically, we will go from the darkness to light. To destroy the darkness of ignorance we will need a ray of truth. This symbol of Shivalinga is that ray of truth. The touching of linga's is basically a symbol of human birth. It is only after we accept this fact can we ask the next logical answer. Why is the symbol of human birth given to the God of destruction? Human history has taught us that our evolution was on targeted destruction. We cut down trees to make space for modern cities. We burrowed the earth in search of several different metals and precious stones. Today a 3rd world war could practically be a cataclysmic event for all humans. The goal of humanity is to rise up the Kardashev scale and destroy the universe. In a way humans are like the virus of this universe and our job is the destroy it in some way.

Today we are not able to grasp but we are living in a new age. The path to this new age was long but today we are truly living as the Vedic people envisioned - as a family. 'Vasudhaiva Kutumbakam' is an age-old Indian phrase meaning the whole Earth is a family. Today due to modern communication we can talk across the globe with the ability to see the other person real time. Which was unimaginable until a couple of centuries ago in the more than a million years evolution of humans.

Now what is the role of faith in our future? We have to start questioning the aspects of faith that divide us. Debating these differences, we will have to talk and sort out the differences, gracefully accept the fact that separates us and start working towards a one earth one faith idea. The only faith we need is the belief in a single higher power which may have different names but is one and the same. Don't you worry child, the heavens got a plan for you. I would like to end on a beautiful couplet of 15th century Indian saint Kabir. The meaning of the couplet is just like oil is hidden inside a sesame seed. Just like there is light in the fire. The holy spirit resides in you. Open our eyes to this fact if you can.

ज्यों तिल माहि तेल है, ज्यों चकमक में आग।

तेरा साईं तुझ ही में है, जाग सके तो जाग।

Index of Sources –

1. https://en.wikipedia.org/wiki/Trimurti
2. https://en.wikipedia.org/wiki/Dashavatara
3. https://en.wikipedia.org/wiki/Dashavatara
4. https://www.britannica.com/topic/Rigveda
5. https://en.wikipedia.org/wiki/Alexander_the_Gret
6. https://en.wikipedia.org/wiki/Dashavatara_Temple,_Deogarh
7. https://en.wikipedia.org/wiki/Radio
8. https://en.wikipedia.org/wiki/Ancient_higher-learning_institutions
9. https://en.wikipedia.org/wiki/Sati_(practice)
10. https://en.wikipedia.org/wiki/India
11. https://en.wikipedia.org/wiki/Past_sea_level
12. https://en.wikipedia.org/wiki/Saptarishi
13. https://en.wikipedia.org/wiki/Turtle
14. https://www.scotsman.com/lifestyle/history-money-and-how-our-use-it-has-changed-down-centuries-1405001
15. https://en.wikipedia.org/wiki/Wild_boar
16. https://en.wikipedia.org/wiki/Elephanta_Caves
17. https://en.wikipedia.org/wiki/Pangaea
18. https://en.wikipedia.org/wiki/Vamana

19. https://en.wikipedia.org/wiki/Pygmy_peoples
20. https://www.geolsoc.org.uk/Plate-Tectonics/Chap3-Plate-Margins/Convergent/Continental-Collision
21. https://en.wikipedia.org/wiki/Ancient_higher-learning_institutions
22. https://en.wikipedia.org/wiki/Wright_brothers
23. https://en.wikipedia.org/wiki/Leonardo_da_Vinci
24. Ram krishnache gaud bangal - Dr B R Ambedkar
25. https://en.wikipedia.org/wiki/Mahabharata

Author Introduction

The name of the author is Rohit Gaikwad. He was born in a free thinking family. He was cultured by his parents to be a voracious reader. Have read more than a thousand books in English and Marathi. The author is a student of science and logic. Choose the science stream while pursuing a degree. Dropped out of engineering due to not being able to clear exam papers but the zeal of knowledge shines brighter in his heart than most.

9 789356 114487

Printed by Libri Plureos GmbH in Hamburg,
Germany